To David Reuther

Little, Brown and Company

Hachette Book Group USA ❁ 237 Park Avenue, New York, NY 10017 ❁ Visit our Web site at www.lb-kids.com

First Edition: September 2007

Library of Congress Cataloging-in-Publication Data

Pinkney, Jerry.
Little Red Riding Hood / written and illustrated by Jerry Pinkney. — 1st ed.
    p. cm.
Summary: A sweet little girl meets a hungry wolf in the forest while on her way to visit her grandmother.
ISBN-13: 978-0-316-01355-0 / ISBN-10: 0-316-01355-2
[1. Fairy tales. 2. Folklore — Germany.] I. Little Red Riding Hood. English. II. Title.
PZ8.P575Lit 2007   398.2 — dc22
[E]   2006025291

10 9 8 7 6 5 4 3 2

TWP   Printed in Singapore

The full-color artwork for this book has been prepared using pencil, watercolor, gouache, and ink on paper.
The text was set in Cochin.

LITTLE, BROWN AND COMPANY
New York ❧ Boston

JERRY PINKNEY

Little Red Riding Hood

In a small cottage there lived a sweet little girl and her dear mother, who once made for her daughter a lovely red riding hood. The child cherished it and wore it everywhere, so that all in the village affectionately called her "Little Red Riding Hood."

One day, Mother cooked some delicious chicken soup and raisin muffins. "Your grandmother is not well today," she told her daughter as she packed the warm treats. "Go see how she is faring. Mind you, little miss," she instructed. "Be certain to go straight there."

Little Red Riding Hood set out at once. The gentle sounds of the child's footsteps in the new snow —*crunch, crunch*—kept her company. "Oh, how peaceful," she thought, catching a snowflake on the tip of her tongue. "I wonder if Grandmama will be surprised to see me."

By and by, Little Red Riding Hood met a sly wolf. The wolf, who was always hungry, had a mind to eat her up at once—but he thought better of it when he heard the *chop, chop* of woodcutters working nearby.

"Where are you going, little one?" he asked in his most pleasant voice.

"My grandmama is not well today," Little Red Riding Hood replied, forgetting that her mother did not want her to delay. "I'm taking her some chicken soup and raisin muffins."

The clever creature smiled. "Does she live far from here?" he asked.

"No," said Little Red Riding Hood. "Just behind the mill, across from the pond, next to the big oak tree."

"I'll join you, for I was just heading that way," said the wolf. He walked along with the child for a short distance and then had an idea. "Why not collect kindling for a fire?" he suggested. "It will warm your granny's heart."

"That's a wonderful idea," said the child. "Look, the snow has brought down many small branches. They will make a good fire."

Little Red Riding Hood gathered as many twigs as she could carry, tying the bundle with the ribbon that had fastened Grandmother's basket.

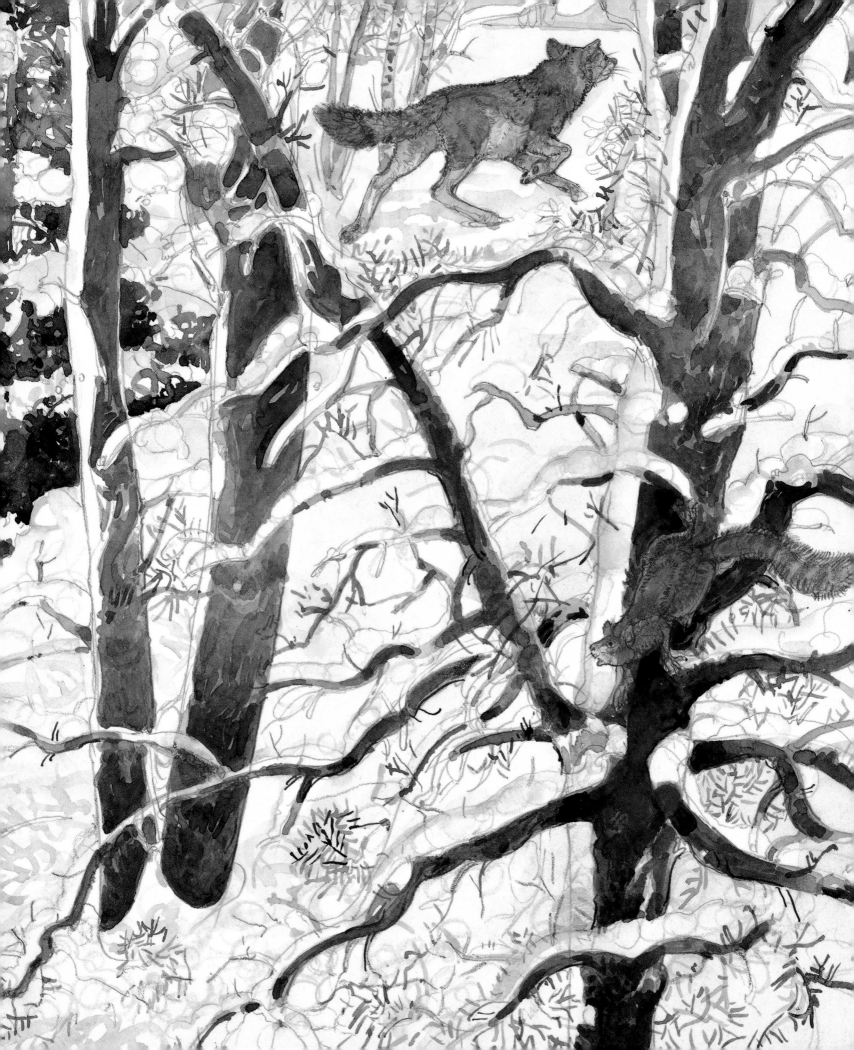

In the meantime, the cunning wolf slipped away to Grandmother's cottage with great haste. *Tap*, *tap*, he knocked.

"Who's there?" asked Grandmother in a frail voice.

"It's me, your granddaughter," replied the crafty scoundrel, doing his very best to sound like a young girl.

"The door is unlocked," Grandmother responded. "Just lift the latch."

Once inside, the wolf leaped upon the startled woman and gobbled her down whole. Then he shut the door and dressed himself in one of Grandmother's nightgowns.

After struggling to get her cap down over his ears, the wolf, who was still quite hungry, settled into the bed to wait for his next meal.

Before long, Little Red Riding Hood arrived at the cottage. *Tap*, *tap*, she knocked.

"Who's there?" croaked the wolf.

The girl was startled by the hoarseness of Grandmother's voice. "It's me, your granddaughter," she responded. "I've brought you soup and Mama's special raisin muffins. And I've found kindling to start a fire. Soon you'll feel just like yourself again!"

"Just lift the latch and come in," the voice invited her. "I can't wait to see how much you've grown."

The little girl opened the door and closed it gently behind her. The wolf lay in bed with the sheets right up to his whiskers and Grandmother's nightcap pulled as low as he could manage.

"Put your basket on the chair, and come closer," he said as sweetly as he could. "You're a head taller since I saw you last."

Little Red Riding Hood, anxious about Grandmother's poor health, went right to her bedside.

"Oh Grandmama, what great arms you have!" said the child in wonder.
"All the better to hug you with, my dear," replied the wolf.
"Oh Grandmama, what great ears you have!" she remarked.
"All the better to hear you with, my dear," the wolf responded.

"Oh Grandmama, what great eyes you have!" the girl cried out.
"All the better to see you with, my dear," declared the wolf.
"Oh Grandmama, what great teeth you have!" she squealed.
"All the better to EAT you with, my dear!" howled the wolf.

With those awful words, the wolf leaped out from under the covers, sprang upon Little Red Riding Hood, and swallowed her whole.

"Now," said the wolf with a satisfied sigh, "a long nap is all I need after such a full meal." And so he climbed back into bed and fell asleep.

The wretched creature snored so loudly that one of the woodcutters, who was passing by the cottage, wondered if something might be wrong with the kindly old woman who lived there.

As the man approached her door, he spotted two sets of fresh tracks in the snow, leading right to the front steps. "One set is that of a small child," he thought. "The second set appears to be large paw prints!"

With one stroke of his ax, he killed the wolf. Then he cut open the animal's stomach with the old woman's sewing shears.

Out jumped Little Red Riding Hood with a smile as bright as fresh snow. Then out climbed the kindly old woman. Once she saw that her granddaughter was out of harm's way, her heart was filled with gratitude. Grandmother had never felt better.

Later, after the woodcutter had buried the wicked wolf in the deep forest, he returned to warm himself by the fireplace, where Grandmother had started a fire with Little Red Riding Hood's kindling. All three were comforted with Mother's chicken soup and raisin muffins. The sweet raisins reminded the girl of home, and of what her mother had told her.

As Little Red Riding Hood readied herself to leave, Grandmother said, "Now, little miss, you be certain to go straight home." And she did.